J
599.
74
Bar

Bare, Colleen
Stanley.
Elephants on the
beach

DATE DUE

1/90

Elephants on the Beach

ELEPHANTS

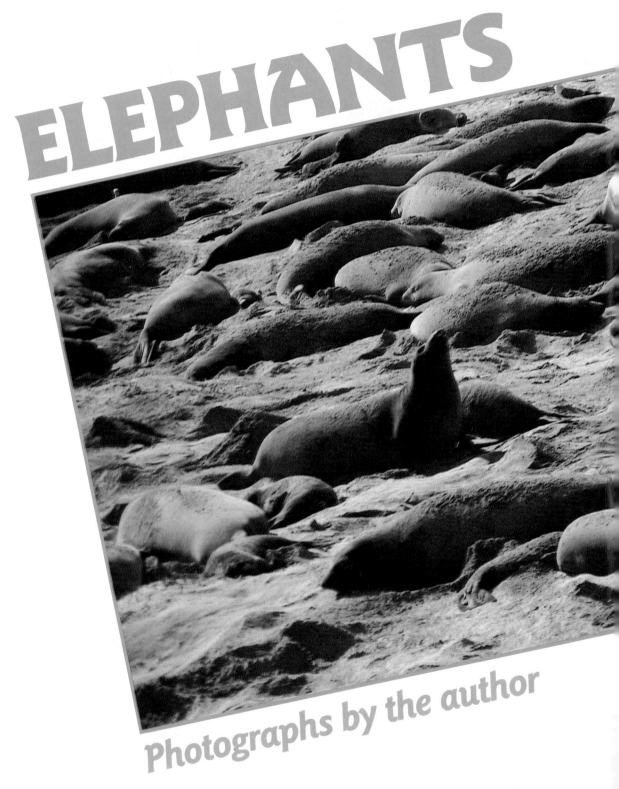

Photographs by the author

on the Beach
Colleen Stanley Bare

Cobblehill Books / Dutton   New York

To Randall

Library of Congress Cataloging-in-Publication Data

Bare, Colleen Stanley.
   Elephants on the beach/Colleen Stanley Bare;
photographs by the author.
      p.   cm.
   Includes index.
   Summary: Text and photographs introduce a seal
whose large nose earns it the name elephant seal.
   ISBN 0-525-65018-0
   1. Elephant seals—Juvenile literature. [1. Elephant
seals.   2. Seals (Animals)] I. Title.
QL737.P64B37 1990
599.74′8—dc20   89-32267
                                                  CIP
                                                  AC

Published in the United States by E. P. Dutton, New
York, N.Y., a division of Penguin Books USA Inc.
Published simultaneously in Canada by Fitzhenry
& Whiteside Limited, Toronto

Designer: Charlotte Staub
Printed in Hong Kong
First edition 10 9 8 7 6 5 4 3 2 1

Real
elephants

Elephant on the beach

Elephants that live on the beach
    and in the sea
are big, like real elephants,
and some have large noses, like real elephants.
This is why their names are nearly the same.

But elephants that live on the beach
    and in the sea
aren't real elephants at all.
They are seals, called *elephant seals*.

5

Elephant seals spend much of their beach time sleeping.

They sleep alone on the sand.

They sleep with others in groups on the sand.

They sleep in hollows scooped out in the sand.

They sleep in shallow water on wet sand.

While they sleep, elephant seals belch, gurgle, groan, snore, sneeze, snort, and when awakened by another seal or human, they may roar as though to say, "Go away, go away."

Many birds share the seals' beach.

Two kinds of elephant seals are found in the sea
and on islands and beaches:
The northern elephant seal along the Pacific
Coast from Mexico to California,
and the southern elephant seal in the
Antarctic.
Both kinds look and act alike, except the
Antarctic seals are a little larger with
shorter snouts.

Elephant seals stay in the sea for over half of
each year, eating, swimming, and sleeping.
They are swift swimmers and deep divers (to
2,000 feet)
and hunt for their food in the ocean,
especially small fish and squid.

Their large seal eyes, for seeing,
and their sensitive, bristly whiskers, for feeling,
help them find fish in the dark, deep waters.

Elephant seals have four flippers.
The rear ones are used for swimming;
the front ones are used for steering and
walking.

Front flipper

On land, elephant seals look clumsy.
They drag themselves across the beaches on
    their bellies,
    and up and down sand dunes,
pulled along by their front flippers.
Their tracks show where they have been.

Their noses have special nostrils that close
    tightly when they are asleep,
so the seals won't drown while sleeping in
    the sea.
They can hold their breaths for about thirty
    minutes underwater.

Elephant seals hear well,
but their tiny ear holes don't show.

No visible ear

Sea lion's visible ear

Among seals, only sea lions and fur seals
have ears that you can see.

Elephant seal skull

Elephant seals have thirty teeth.
Grown-ups have large-sized teeth.

Pups have small-sized teeth.

The air is filled with sand near elephant seals.
They flip sand over their bodies,
   probably to keep cool.

They cover themselves with sand blankets.

Among elephant seals:
Males are *bulls*—
   up to eighteen feet and six thousand pounds.
Females are *cows*—
   up to twelve feet and two thousand pounds.
Babies are *pups*—
   newborns up to five feet and ninety pounds.

Only bulls have big noses,
that grow as the bulls grow,
to about two feet at age nine.

Cow noses stay small compared to bull noses.

There are many different looking noses on the beach…

smaller younger noses

larger older noses

growing
rounded
noses

big bloated, bumpy noses

rough, scarred, beaten-up noses

In winter, elephant seals go ashore on West
      Coast beaches, to breed and to mate.
Bulls arrive first, soon followed by the cows.

Bulls roar at other bulls through their huge
      noses,
and they fight.

They slash at each other with their sharp teeth,
until the biggest and strongest chase away the
losers.
Victorious bulls become the beachmasters,
also named *alpha bulls*.
They guard and protect a group of up to fifty
cows, called *harems*.

Bull and harem

Within a few days after her arrival on the beach,
each cow gives birth to one black-coated,
    woolly pup
that she nurses for four weeks.
The pups gain about ten pounds a day.

Cows and pups

After the nursing period, mother cows mate
    with a beachmaster
and then return to the ocean to feed,
leaving the pups to care for themselves.

A weaner

A superweaner

Now the pups are called *weaners*,
because they are weaned from their mothers'
  milk.

A few pups manage to nurse from two mothers.
They grow very fat and are called
  superweaners.

Bulls and cows

Each beachmaster bull guards his harem
  of cows,
fights off other bulls,
and goes without food or water for three
  months.
He returns to the ocean after the cows
  have left.

The weaners don't go to sea for another two
  months.
They sleep and practice swimming.

A weaner

Once a year, in the warm months,
elephant seals return to the beaches for about
    four weeks.
They return to lie on the sand and "molt,"
    meaning

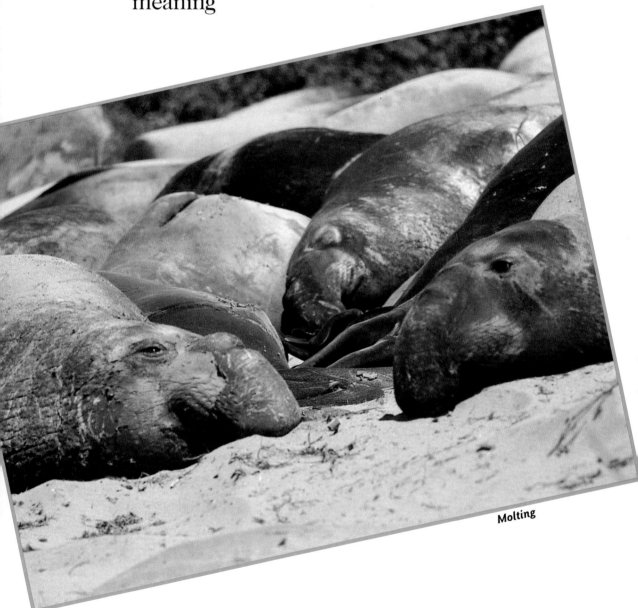

Molting

New fur

they shed their fur coats and outer layers of
    skin,
which are replaced by new skin and new fur.

Elephant seals can live fifteen years,
but they have enemies: killer whales, large
sharks, and man.
In the 1800s, humans killed most of the world's
elephant seals,
to use their fat (*blubber*) for oil.
Now laws protect the seals.

But seals aren't protected from pollution, oil
spills, or from plastic thrown in the ocean by
careless humans.
The scar on this seal's neck was from a plastic
band.

Some day you may visit an elephant seal beach,
but don't get too close to the seals,
    because they might bite.
Just watch and enjoy these fascinating,
    magnificent elephants of the beach
    and the sea.

The Seal Story

All seals belong to a scientific group called PINNIPEDIA (PINN-I-PE-DIA). This is a Latin word meaning "fin-footed." Within this group are three Pinniped families.

Phocidae—the "earless" seals, also called "true" seals, which include the elephant seals.

Otariidae—the "eared" seals which are only the sea lions and fur seals.

Odobenidae—consists of just the walrus, which is also earless.

Index